# I Think it's a Monster!

Written by Katie Foufouti

Illustrated by Fran and David Brylewski

## Collins

# Who's in this story?

Listen and say

Download the audio at www.collins.co.uk/839827

Rob

Miranda

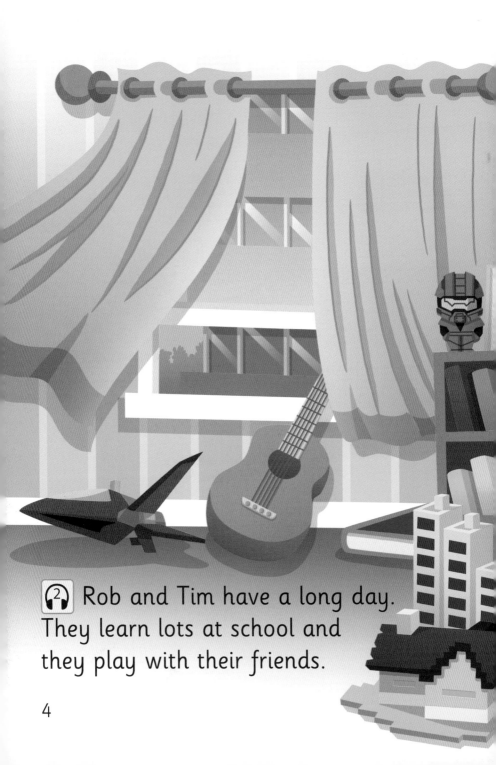

🎧 Rob and Tim have a long day.
They learn lots at school and
they play with their friends.

4

After school, they play football. Then Rob takes his skateboard to the park and Tim plays the guitar. They do a lot.

In the morning, the boys wake up
for school. Tim is getting dressed.

"It's some soil," says Tim. But how
did it get there? Rob went to the park
after school. Was it soil from his shoe?

There's no time to think about the soil. The boys need to go to school. They have a lot to do today.

After school, Rob and Tim sometimes play a sport, sometimes go shopping and sometimes play video games.

Before dinner, the brothers are playing in their bedroom. Then Tim finds some grass on the floor.

They look out of the window.

"Did it come in with the wind?" asks Rob.

"It's a beautiful sunny afternoon, and there's no wind." says Tim.

"Dinner!" calls Dad. The boys stop thinking about the grass. They're hungry at the end of the day.

But when they go to their bedroom after dinner ...

... they find more grass!

Who put the grass there? Rob thinks it was Tim.

At school, Tim tells his friend Fred about the soil and the grass.

"Were they in your bedroom?" asks Fred.

"Yes, they were on the floor," says Tim.

Fred thinks a monster lives in their bedroom. It comes out when the brothers aren't there.

"The monster put the soil and the grass on the floor," says Fred.

At home, Tim looks for the monster. "There's nothing here," he says.

Rob looks at floor. "Look at these feathers!" he says.

Cousin Miranda is here. She sometimes takes the train to the city.
The boys show Miranda the feathers.

Miranda looks out of the window.
She looks down. She looks up. Then she
sees a bird. It's making a nest.

"We thought it was a monster, but it was a swallow!" says Tim.

"Look at the nest!" says Rob.

It's Saturday. The boys are at home and they've got their dad's selfie stick and their mum's phone.

They want to see the nest!

The mother swallow isn't in the nest.
It's looking for food. The baby birds
are very hungry!

"Let's send the photos to Miranda!"
says Tim.

# Picture dictionary

Listen and repeat

feather

grass

nest

selfie stick

soil

sunny

swallow

# 1 Look and order the story

# 2 Listen and say

# Collins

Published by Collins
An imprint of HarperCollins*Publishers*
Westerhill Road
Bishopbriggs
Glasgow
G64 2QT

HarperCollins*Publishers*
1st Floor, Watermarque Building
Ringsend Road
Dublin 4
Ireland

William Collins' dream of knowledge for all began with the publication of his first book in 1819.

A self-educated mill worker, he not only enriched millions of lives, but also founded a flourishing publishing house. Today, staying true to this spirit, Collins books are packed with inspiration, innovation and practical expertise. They place you at the centre of a world of possibility and give you exactly what you need to explore it.

10 9 8 7 6 5 4 3 2

ISBN 978-0-00-839827-9

www.collins.co.uk/elt

British Library Cataloguing in Publication Data

A catalogue record for this publication is available from the British Library.

Author: Katie Foufouti
Illustrator: Fran and David Brylewski (Beehive)
Series editor: Rebecca Adlard
Commissioning editor: Fiona Undrill
Publishing manager: Lisa Todd
Product managers: Jennifer Hall and Caroline Green
In-house editor: Alma Puts Keren
Project manager: Emily Hooton
Editor: Matthew Hancock
Proofreaders: Natalie Murray and Michael Lamb
Cover designer: Kevin Robbins
Typesetter: 2Hoots Publishing Services Ltd
Audio produced by id audio, London
Reading guide author: Emma Wilkinson
Production controller: Rachel Weaver
Printed and bound by: GPS Group, Slovenia

Download the audio for this book and a reading guide for parents and teachers at www.collins.co.uk/839827